D0997824

For Lilya

First published in 2008
by Meadowside Children's Books
185 Fleet Street London EC4A 2HS
www.meadowsidebooks.com

Text and illustrations © Daniel Postgate 2008
The right of Daniel Postgate to be identified
as the author and illustrator has been asserted
by him in accordance with the Copyright,
Designs and Patents Act, 1988

A CIP catalogue record for this book
is available from the British Library

10 9 8 7 6 5 4 3 2 1
Printed in Indonesia

THERE'S A YETI IN MY SHED!

Daniel Postgate

meadowside
CHILDREN'S BOOKS

There's a yeti in our potting shed.
I can't believe my eyes.
I never thought you'd get a yeti
In a shed that size.

He's peeping out the window.
I better not go out.
I think it's best to stay indoors
When yetis are about!

He's climbing out
the door now.

He's stretching
with a yawn.

He's scratching at his belly and
He's coming down the lawn!

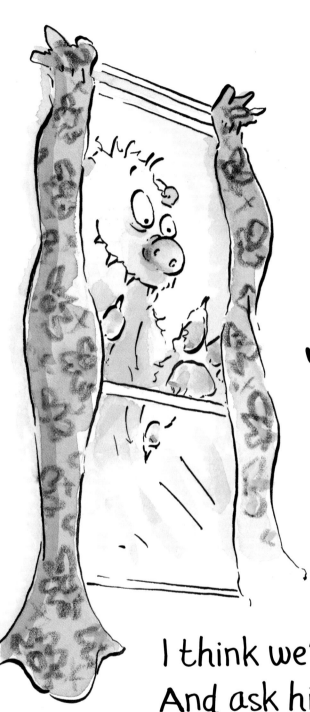

I quickly tell my father.
He answers, "Are you sure?
We've never had a yeti
In the potting shed before."

He takes a look and says,
"You're right!
Well goodness gracious me.

I think we'd better be polite
And ask him in for tea."

We sit him at the table
With napkin, fork and knife.
I've never seen a yeti
Eat so much in all my life.

He has:
Noodles, fish pie, chocolate cake,
Strudels, French-fries, rib-eye steak,
Truffle, offal, muffin, waffle,
Cherry slice and cream.

Chicken curry (very hot)
And when he's finished off the lot,
He drinks straight
  from the coffee pot
And licks the dishes clean.

Straight up the garden path we head

And hide inside
the potting shed
until the
screaming
stops.

At last mum says, "Alright, okay
Your friend seems nice enough...
He can stay, just for today."
I yell, "Yippee, yahoo, hooray!"
And take my new friend off to play
All sorts of crazy stuff.

He's very good at hide and seek
Which came as some surprise because
I thought I'd find him easily,
Considering the size he was!

He's champion at twisting,
Even beats my great aunt Sue.

Then joins my little sister in
A game of peek-a-boo!

Then bouncing on the trampoline
We get to quite a
height!

The yeti waves a hairy paw
And makes a very scary "ROAR"
Which gives poor Mr Brown next door
A rather nasty fright!

We have a game of Mister Wolf,
Now that is REALLY FUN!
And when he shouts out

"DINNER TIME!"

You should have seen us run!

Just then, we hear a growling sound;
Like rumbling thunder rolling round.
A darkness falls across the ground,
And blots the evening sun.

We all look up, quite terrified,
And see a beast before our eyes,

A creature of
enormous size...

It is the Yeti's mUm!

"my lovely boy," the monster roars,
"Don't wander off alone.
I've told you many times before,
You stay with me.
You're only four!"

And then she takes him by the paw and quickly heads for home.

I watch him go, my yeti friend,
Until he's out of sight.

I hope one day he'll come again
And maybe stay the night.

Next day, a card lies in the hall
Addressed to 'Everyone'.
I open it and read the scrawl;
It's from the Yeti's mum...

My son had such a lovely play,
He was as pleased as punch!
You must come 'round
our cave some day...